MISSION:
BACK TO SCHOOL

For Paul,
elementary teacher *extraordinaire*!
—S.H.

For Mom and Dad
—M.L.

Text copyright © 2016 by Susan Hood
Jacket art and interior illustrations copyright © 2016 by Mary Lundquist

Visit us on the Web! randomhousekids.com

Educators and librarians, for a variety of teaching tools, visit us at RHTeachersLibrarians.com

Library of Congress Cataloging-in-Publication Data
Hood, Susan, author.
Mission: back to school : top-secret information / by Susan Hood ; illustrated by Mary Lundquist. — First edition.
pages cm
Summary: Imagined in the form of a secret agent's set of instructions, Mason and other children negotiate the first day of school.
ISBN 978-0-385-38471-1 (hardcover) — ISBN 978-0-375-97349-9 (hardcover library binding) — ISBN 978-0-385-38472-8 (ebook)
1. First day of school—Juvenile fiction. 2. Elementary schools—Juvenile fiction. [1. First day of school—Fiction. 2. Schools—
Fiction.] I. Lundquist, Mary, illustrator. II. Title.
PZ7.H763315Mg 2016 813.54—dc23 [E] 2015013850

Book design by John Sazaklis

MANUFACTURED IN CHINA
10 9 8 7 6 5 4 3 2 1
First Edition

MISSION: BACK TO SCHOOL

WRITTEN BY
SUSAN HOOD

ILLUSTRATED BY
MARY LUNDQUIST

TOP-SECRET INFORMATION

Random House 🏠 New York

CLASSIFIED INFORMATION

It's time. Time for the first day of school!

Your mission?

To begin the first phase of training

in your hunt for intelligence.

We know you're up for the challenge!

Are you ready?

START HERE.

#1. SUIT UP.

#2. RENDEZVOUS AT VEHICLE CHECKPOINT.

#3.
MEET INTELLIGENCE OFFICER.

#4.
UNPACK GEAR.

SUBMIT
CASE FILES.

#5. BUILD DIPLOMATIC RELATIONS.

#6.
GATHER FOR DEBRIEFING.

#9.
DEVELOP SECRET SIGNALS.

MAY I GO TO
THE BATHROOM?

SOMETHING SMELLS STINKY!

I DON'T KNOW.

QUIET DOWN, PLEASE.

I KNOW THE ANSWER.
I HAVE A QUESTION.

TIME OUT.

GOOD JOB!

#11. CONDUCT FIELDWORK.

SWALLOW THE EVIDENCE.

#13.
DEVELOP LINES OF COMMUNICATION.

COLLECT FINGERPRINTS.

#14. CONDUCT PHYSICAL TRAINING EXERCISES.

GO UNDERCOVER.

HOLD HIGH-LEVEL
MEETINGS.

#15.
UNCOVER
INFORMATION.

CHECK OUT COUNTER-INTELLIGENCE.

#16. COVER YOUR TRACKS.

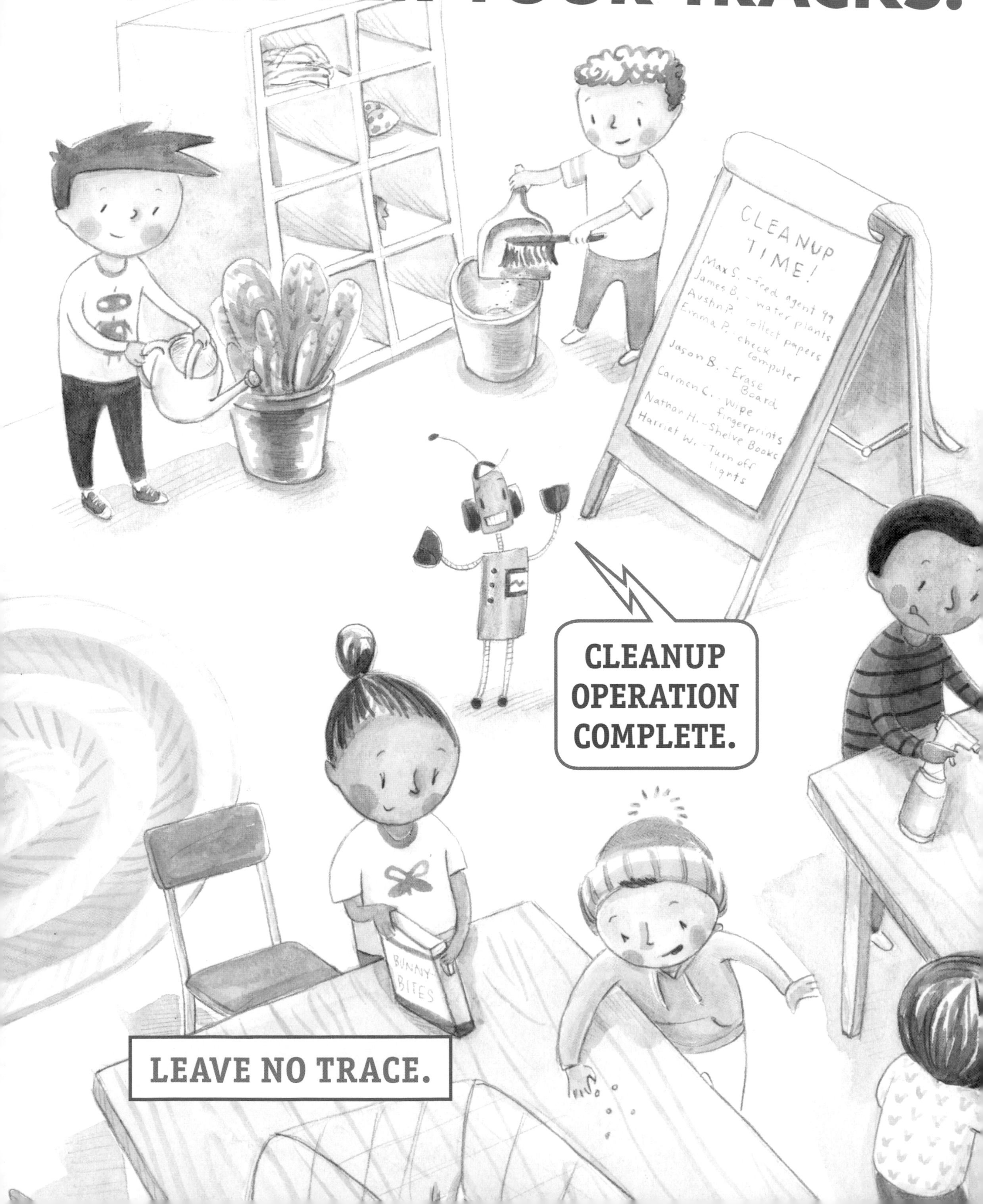

#17. RETURN TO HEADQUARTERS.

#18.
SHARE TOP-SECRET INFORMATION.